UNDER THE STAIRS

UNDER THE STAIRS

Fiona Dunbar

RED FOX

For Ross William

Sophie hated Sunday afternoons at Aunt Sarah's. There was nothing to play with and nothing to do except listen to the grown-ups drone on and on.

'Don't touch that, dear,' said Aunt Sarah. 'Why don't you go upstairs and play with the cat?'

But instead of going *up* the stairs, Sophie went *under* them!

Under the stairs was as dark as night. Sophie found a torch and switched it on.

'Oh,' she sighed. 'Nothing but a load of old junk.'

But her torch shone like a moon and the world under the stairs began to stir in its light.

First a group of brush-like creatures shook out their dusty bristles and clambered out of their nest.

'BRUSH-HOGS!' sang Sophie as the bristly creatures scampered all around and began to play.

Then the TENNISWELLIES stretched their limbs and creaked across the floor to introduce themselves. While in the corner...

…the GOLFLOGOG wiggled his stumpy legs like an upside-down beetle. 'Help me, *please*,' he wailed. 'I'm stuck the wrong way round!'

'Don't listen to him,' said the Tenniswellies. 'It's a trick.'
But it was too late.

As soon as he was on his feet the Golflogog snorted with laughter, opened his mouth, and fired a shower of golf balls at them.

Behind them the GARDEN-CHAIR HORSE swished her tail and stamped her hooves. 'Hop on, quick,' she called. Sophie leapt astride.

As they rode to safety there was a great *whoosh* as a flock of DUSTERBIRDS took to the air. 'Snichoo! Snichoo!' they went.

'It's raining sneezes!' cried Sophie.

   'Shhhhhh,' whispered the Garden-chair horse, slowing to a trot. 'We must be careful not to wake the...'

Before she could finish they heard a low 'Hummmmmmmmmmmm.'
A terrifying HOOVERSAURUS stood in their path!

'Hummmmmmmmmmmm. Hummmmmmmmmmmm,' it moaned, swaying its big
neck from side to side.

'Out of the way,' yelled Sophie, thrusting it back with her umbrella-sword.

But the Hooversaurus just snatched up the umbrella-sword in its powerful jaws and began to eat it.

'Hey!' cried Sophie. Suddenly everything went very quiet.

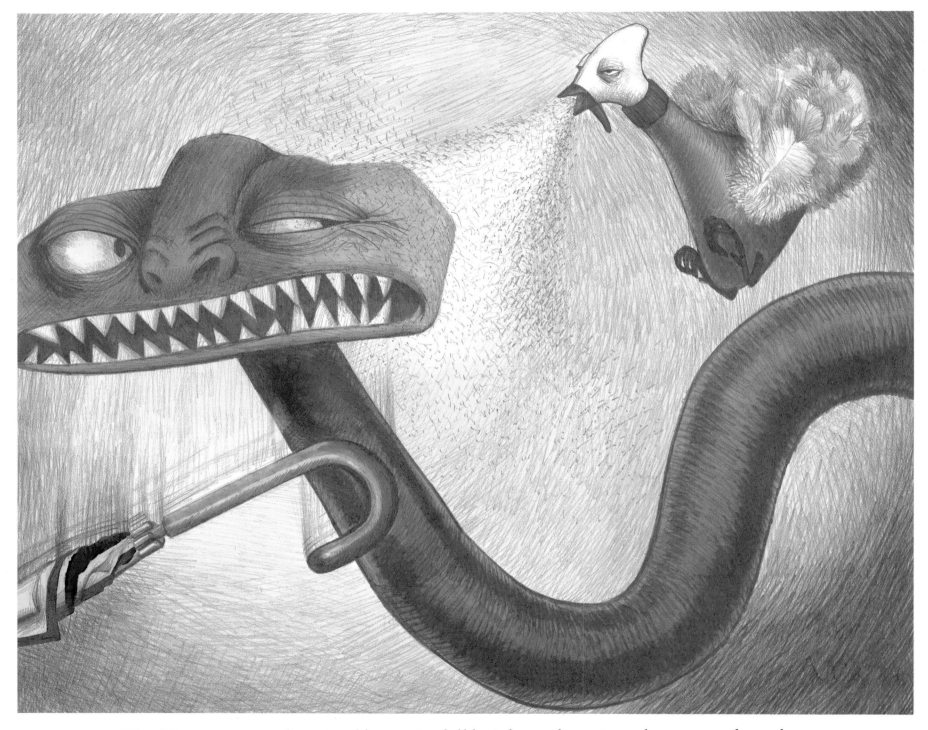

The Hooversaurus drew itself up to its full height and was just about to strike, when – 'Snichoooo!' went a Dusterbird.
And if there's one thing a Hooversaurus *hates* it is being sneezed at.

It swung this way and that, that way and this and tied its neck up in a great big knot.
'Help me, *please*,' it croaked. But Sophie wasn't being caught a second time.

From somewhere outside she heard the sound of footsteps and Mum's voice calling, 'S-o-p-h-i-e!'.

'Time to go,' said Sophie sadly. 'But I'll be back next Sunday.'

The little door opened and a familiar face appeared. 'Hurry up,' said the TABBY CAT, 'they're leaving.'

Sophie scrambled out just in time.

'I hope you weren't bored,' said Mum on the way out.

'Not *too* bored,' said Sophie, smiling to herself. Sunday afternoons at Aunt Sarah's would never ever be the same again.

A Red Fox Book

Published by Random House Children's Books
20 Vauxhall Bridge Road, London SW1V 2SA.

A division of Random House UK Ltd
London Melbourne Sydney Auckland
Johannesburg and agencies throughout the world

Copyright © Fiona Dunbar 1993

1 3 5 7 9 10 8 6 4 2

First published in Great Britain 1993
by Hutchinson Children's Books

Red Fox edition 1995

Printed in China

RANDOM HOUSE UK Limited Reg. No. 954009

ISBN 0 09 916511 2

Some bestselling Red Fox picture books

THE BIG ALFIE AND ANNIE ROSE STORYBOOK
by Shirley Hughes
OLD BEAR
by Jane Hissey
OI! GET OFF OUR TRAIN
by John Burningham
DON'T DO THAT!
by Tony Ross
NOT NOW, BERNARD
by David McKee
ALL JOIN IN
by Quentin Blake
THE WHALES' SONG
by Gary Blythe and Dyan Sheldon
JESUS' CHRISTMAS PARTY
by Nicholas Allan
THE PATCHWORK CAT
by Nicola Bayley and William Mayne
MATILDA
by Hilaire Belloc and Posy Simmonds
WILLY AND HUGH
by Anthony Browne
THE WINTER HEDGEHOG
by Ann and Reg Cartwright
A DARK, DARK TALE
by Ruth Brown
HARRY, THE DIRTY DOG
by Gene Zion and Margaret Bloy Graham
DR XARGLE'S BOOK OF EARTHLETS
by Jeanne Willis and Tony Ross
WHERE'S THE BABY?
by Pat Hutchins